THE MOST DELICIOUS
CAMPING TRIP EVER

THE MOST DELICIOUS CAMPING TRIP EVER

by Alice Bach

Pictures by Steven Kellogg

Harper & Row, Publishers
New York, Hagerstown, San Francisco, London

Library of Congress Cataloging in Publication Data
Bach, Alice.
    The most delicious camping trip ever.

    SUMMARY: Ronald and Oliver, the bear twins,
go camping with Aunt Bear and learn to get along
with nature and each other.
        [1. Camping—Fiction.   2. Bears—Fiction]
I. Kellogg, Steven.   II.   Title.
PZ7.B1314Mr3   [E]   76-2956
ISBN 0-06-020338-2
ISBN 0-06-020339-0 lib. bdg.

For Erica and Jon,
because this bear loves you

"Ronald, what is this jumble?" Ma pointed to his bed.

"What I haven't organized yet." He looked down at his list. "Tree-identification book, packet of straight pins, two small jars. You have to punch holes in the lids, Ma, so the specimens get enough air—"

Ma cut through his explanation. "What is that heap on the floor?"

"Equipment. Cotton swabs, magnifying glass, ball of heavy string, notebook, and—" He held up several pencils bound with a rubber band. Ma had her waiting look.

Calmly Ronald put down his bunch of pencils.

"To participate in a scientific expedition, you need the proper equipment," said Ronald.

"I'm sure you do. But this is only a twenty-four-hour camping trip—just you, Oliver, and Aunt Bear."

"It may be a plain camping trip for them, but for me it's practice—my first field trip." He looked straight into Ma's eyes. "I may leave for the South Pole or Africa soon." He pointed to each item. "Small jars for insects, this fat one for butterflies"—he reached for a net and swooshed it around Ma's legs—"to catch the butterflies, see?" He squatted next to his pile.

"This room is cluttered enough. No more creatures. Especially for experiments. You remember what Pa told you after the turtle?"

"Ma, it's normal to investigate what's under their shells."

Ma smiled. "Don't capture any crocodiles!"

"Do you think we'll see any?" Ronald jumped up.

"No, you silly bear. Roll up your sleeping bag, clean up this mess, and don't forget your

toothbrush." Ma clapped her paws together.
"Hurry now."

Ronald shook his head and tried to capture
his bird book with the butterfly net.

Ronald's twin, Oliver, was standing on a chair, poking among the boxes stacked on the top shelf of his closet.

"What are you doing?"

"I can't find my muffin pans." Oliver sighed. "After we gather a pail of plump, juicy, purple berries, we'll want to bake muffins. Ma, do you have a tiny something that would hold a few tablespoons of baking powder?"

"Oliver, you're going to camp outdoors, to forage for food in the woods and meadows, not to a course in home economics."

"What are we going to eat?" He frowned.

"Nothing, if you and Ronald keep fooling around. Aunt Bear will be here any minute. Oliver, no muffin pans. Now hurry!"

"Ma, I am hurrying. I've been hurrying for hours." He butted Ma's stomach lightly, inching her out of his room.

After slipping a small jar of cinnamon sticks and a couple of handfuls of cloves into the zipper compartment of his sleeping bag, he said to himself, "I wonder where those ginger candies went." He walked into Ronald's room. "You seen my ginger candies?"

"I hate ginger candies. They burn my tongue." Ronald was polishing his magnifying glass gently with a soft rag.

"You excited about this trip?"

"As long as we have to go, I plan to collect as much data as possible."

"Data, like dates?" Oliver's eyes gleamed.

"No, like insects, butterflies, snails—"

"To eat?"

"No, you fool. To study. To observe. Here in the laboratory."

"How do you study a butterfly?" Oliver pressed his lips together.

"All I've read so far is you poke a pin through the butterfly after you catch it."

Oliver leaned up against Ronald's fish tank. "You want to poke pins through butterflies? Sounds weird to me." He swung his paw out—straight into the fish tank.

"You can't be trusted in my laboratory. Get your paw away from that angelfish. You'll scare it to death."

"Actually I might prepare it for Frank's supper with a delicious lemon sauce."

"That hamster might be the perfect specimen when I get to the last chapter in my biology correspondence course. Dissecting!"

"What's dissecting?" Oliver asked, wiping his paw on Ronald's bedspread. He might have to hide Frank. From the excited tug Ronald gave his ear, dissecting was not healthy for hamsters.

"Cutting up specimens."

"Keep away from Frank. You know what Pa said after you messed with Katy and Ben." His voice got squeaky. "I loved those little mice."

"Stop whining. It was all in the interest of science."

"Nothing in my room, not one thing, is in the interest of science, or I am going to tell Pa, and you'll get it."

"It'll be a long time before I reach rodents. That's what hamsters are. I skipped most of the middle of the book. That's why the experiment didn't go so well with Katy and Ben."

"You want to go on this hike?" Oliver asked.

Ronald shrugged. "You?"

Oliver sighed deeply. "Aunt Bear is always saying living outdoors means traveling light. And we shouldn't pack much—just a toothbrush and a sleeping bag. No *food*."

"You are right, right, right."

Oliver stretched his eyes wide. "I am?"

Ronald quickly flipped the pages of his bird book. "See how many birds are out there? I bet Aunt Bear doesn't have binoculars."

"You are right, right, right." Oliver shook his head, thinking about muffin pans, a large thermos filled with frosty lemonade, an iron skillet. "Bottle opener. I forgot to pack one."

"What will there be to open?" Ronald asked. "She thinks this trip is a big treat. Finding food in the wild." They both groaned.

"We have to go." They groaned louder.

"We have to make private preparations," Ronald said. "We can't be trapped in the wilderness without proper equipment. Aunt Bear knows zip about biology or any of the other scientific disciplines."

"We don't need science. What we need is food." Oliver smiled, picturing hot blueberry muffins. "And Aunt Bear is a whizbang cook."

"A big help that is. You think she'd haul her stove down to the riverbank to cook us a ten-course dinner?" Ronald tugged angrily on his ear. "Ma says it's only for overnight. But I don't notice her and Pa going along. This may be the worst hike in history."

Chewing his lip, thinking about a whole day and night away from a stove, Oliver tried to smile. "Remember, Aunt Bear's paws are berry-stained. She knows where the most luscious wild grasses grow. And there are nuts, seeds, tree bark, roots—" Oliver looked very sick.

"If—we—can—find—them." Ronald stretched out the words and swished his butterfly net as though to catch each one.

"We might starve," Oliver whispered. He staggered to his feet.

"Where are you going?"

"The kitchen. To pack provisions, hide some fruit, bread, grab cookies, anything! Maybe a jar of peanut butter. In case the meadows and woods have been picked clean by starving campers."

"Sit, Oliver, while I think." Ronald paced back and forth in front of the mirror, one paw cupping his chin. "A *jar* of peanut butter—"

"Most of your ideas end up with us going to bed an hour early for a week." But he listened anyway. Even one of Ronald's ideas was better than a day without food.

"Suppose you pack a *jar* of peanut butter, a *plastic bag* of cookies, Ma's big *thermos* filled with juice—"

"Lemonade."

"Whatever." Ronald spun around in a circle and clutched Oliver's shoulder. "With my help, you'll eat all that stuff, right?"

"But how are we going to keep it a secret? Sneak off and eat in the bushes?"

"Aunt Bear will be so relieved when she sees what a wise move it is, better pack *double*. You know how she is about Ma's cookies. She won't want to hike hungry any more than we do." Ronald stroked his chin. "And I can use the empty jar, bag, and thermos for my specimens."

"It's your best idea ever."

"It is, isn't it?" Ronald took Oliver's arm. "Get moving. And no noise."

"You decoy Ma, OK?"

"Obviously." Ronald watched himself in the mirror, and with a face full of smiles, he called in his baby voice, "Ma, could you come here a minute?"

"Are you ready?" Ma asked.

"You were right, I was taking too much equipment. It's just an overnight hike, not a laboratory on wheels."

Ma settled herself on Ronald's bed. "I'm glad we don't have to squabble on that score. You are lucky Aunt Bear loves the outdoors. I've never liked camping and Pa prefers indoor life too. I remember once all of us set out on a camping trip, couldn't have been much older than you and Oliver. Uncle Otto took us. It started to rain, really *pour,* and there we all were, shivering and miserable. Poor Pa couldn't sleep all night because a huge, gnarled root was digging into his back." Ma smiled.

"What happened?" Ronald asked.

"Nothing. We dried out. But Pa and I decided that indoors was where we wanted to be. I prefer watching lightning storms from a window rather than from a meadow."

"Even when you were little?" Ronald sat at her feet and wrapped his arms around her legs.

"Absolutely! Aunt Bear was always a great one for roaming the woods. I preferred playing house under the piano."

"I bet that was fun, huh Ma?"

"Even when Aunt Bear was still a cub, she could catch fish in her paws. She was so quick in the water, her paws became a blur for those of us on shore."

"In her paws!" Ronald hung on tight.

"I like bright sunflowers, Queen Anne's lace, jack-in-the-pulpit—but I like my flowers in a vase on the table."

"They always look so nice the way you fix them, Ma."

"Where's Oliver? It's too quiet in this house."

"Maybe he's reading. I gave him some of my real easy books."

Ma stood up and untangled herself from Ronald's arms.

Ronald closed his eyes and shouted, "Oliver, Ma's looking for you."

"Here I am." Oliver ran headlong into Ma.

"Here *I* am," called Aunt Bear.

"Come on in, they are ready," Ma answered as she went to greet her sister.

"You get everything?" Ronald muttered out of the side of his mouth.

Oliver nodded. "And a can of tuna, loaf of rye, this plastic bowl of bean salad from last night."

"Perfect. That's a tight-fitting lid. Ideal for a sample of river water."

"There's more. A half-filled crock of strawberry preserves—cuts the sticky problem of pure peanut butter—"

"Terrific. But we've got to stash it fast. Ma will be chasing after us if we don't get out there. Is the crock big enough for a butterfly?"

"Three butterflies!" Oliver said as they divvied up the food.

RONALD'S
OFFICIAL
LABORATORY

NO PESTS ALLOWED

SCIENTISTS
WELCOME

A SMARTLY DRESSED BEAR

"Aunt Bear, here we are." Both bears hugged
their huge aunt.

"What's in your packs?" Ma asked suspi-
ciously.

"Sleeping bags," Oliver said, hoping he didn't
look guilty.

"Toothbrushes, like you told us, and one
book." Ronald waved the butterfly net and
jabbed Oliver, who had closed his eyes.

"Haven't seen one of those in years." Aunt Bear reached for the net.

"It's yours. I found it in the attic with your old stuff."

"You'd better go. You'll miss the sunniest part of the day," Ma said, moving them all toward the door.

"We're very prepared," Ronald and Oliver said happily.

"Have fun and mind Aunt Bear," Ma called as she moved her rocker into a patch of sunlight.

"Speak up if my pace is too fast. Don't want you winded early on." Aunt Bear headed toward the path that wound round the edge of the woods.

"Will there be lots of berries?"

"One way or another, I think I can guarantee a lot of berries."

"Will there be insects?"

"Don't worry, Ronald. I packed plenty of insect repellent." She patted his head.

"No, Aunt Bear. You can't do that. I *want* them for experiments."

"We'll try to work out some accommodation," she answered. "Take rhythmic strides. One-two-left-right. Then your legs won't tire so easily. Even-pace-left-right."

"What's accommodation?" Ronald asked.

"You don't know a word?" Oliver leapt into the air, snatched a pawful of leaves, and sprinkled them on Ronald's head.

"I'll give you an example," said Aunt Bear. "You want insects. Oliver and I don't. So we find a way for you to collect the nasty things and for us not to get bitten or buzzed at."

"I hate bugs, I hate bugs," Oliver sang. He was so happy. Even though his pack felt heavier with every step, it was comforting to know that the peanut-butter jar was rubbing up against the crock of jam.

"You're not going to ruin this expedition just because you don't have a scientific mind. Aunt Bear, tell him bugs are important. Tell him about the balance of nature."

"Bugs are important to those who like them."

"And that's not me or Aunt Bear," Oliver said. "Of course, people who collect bugs have to have something to collect their bugs *in*." Oliver looked up at the balloon-blue sky and lightly punched Ronald's backpack.

Ronald knew Oliver had him. He gritted his teeth and said through squinty eyes, "You win. But after I have collected my specimens, if I happen to find some poisonous thing, say a copperhead snake or a yellow jacket, you'd better start running."

"Stop squabbling. There are no copperheads, first of all. This is the wrong climate for them. And if you try to capture a yellow jacket, little cub, all you're going to collect is a sting that'll swell up twice the size of your paw. Now let's try some accommodating." She took Ronald by the shoulder, put him on her left side, and held Oliver in place on her right.

"Just what do you want to collect, Ronald?"

"Specimens," he said softly.

"Specimens of what?"

"Anything. I need specimens for my mobile laboratory."

"Ah, now I get it. Near the place where we're going to spend the night is a pond covered with waterlilies. They are beautiful, soft pastel colors. They'd be an asset to any laboratory. You could float them in a tank next to the fish."

"That sounds good, but it's not enough."

"What do you really want?"

"I'll know it when I see it. Maybe frogs or snakes?"

"Maybe *a* frog or *a* garter snake. But your ma will not take it kindly if you turn your laboratory into a zoo!"

"Remember the turtle?" Oliver giggled.

"He really was a lot better off in the woods." Aunt Bear ruffled Ronald's fur. "We'll try to accommodate your need for specimens and Ma's rules."

"Oh look!" Oliver gasped. Ronald stopped so fast he pitched forward. Aunt Bear rested her pack on the ground. The meadow in front of them was studded with orange-speckled tiger lilies and daisies. There was no breeze stirring; the scene seemed still like a painting. After a while, Aunt Bear heaved her pack onto her back and said they'd better get a move on or they'd never reach the riverbank by dusk.

"Could we pick some of those flowers?" Ronald pointed to some lavender-blue flowers clustered together. "What are they?"

Aunt Bear thought for a moment. "Purple phlox, or maybe blue phlox, it's slipped my mind. But come here and see these—they're called swamp candles."

"But this isn't a swamp," Ronald said.

"That's their name," Oliver said. "Can we pick them? They look like stars."

"Let's pick a bunch of wildflowers for Ma tomorrow," Aunt Bear said. "They wouldn't last the night out of water. Also, down by the riverbank there are buttercups and some special white violets with downy leaves. She's been partial to those since she was a girl."

"What about accommodation?" Ronald did not like a word he did not know. "I have to be able to use it in a sentence."

"It's a long word for saying we all try to bend a little. You go about collecting your data, Oliver can set up camp and build a fire, and I'll get in a little fishing."

"That sounds simple enough." They agreed.

"It can get tricky if one bear wants a butter-fly and the other one has the net." Aunt Bear looked up at the sky. Ronald and Oliver exchanged worried looks. There was no way she could have guessed.

"Sun's a little past noon. About one o'clock," Aunt Bear said in a totally different voice, as though they hadn't mentioned butterflies or nets or accommodation.

"How can you tell?" Oliver asked.

"Lift one arm straight over your head. That's noon. Now lift your other arm to where the sun is, and you become a clock."

"Hey, it's about one-twenty," Ronald shouted, waving his arms frantically.

"I have a favorite spot. As soon as we get there, we can eat and rest." She readjusted Oliver's pack higher on his shoulders.

In about half an hour—they had to stop every few minutes for Ronald to be a clock—they put down their packs.

"This is another of nature's presents," Aunt Bear said softly. On each side of a small brook grew sprawling rose bushes with fat blooming flowers, their petals in varying shades of pink. Large stones worn smooth by the water made a natural bridge across the brook, which foamed where it slid over the rocks.

"It looks good enough to eat," Oliver said.

The cubs gathered some roses, ouching when they got pricked by the needle-sharp thorns. Aunt Bear rested, her face up—turned to the sun.

Soon they had armfuls of roses, which they heaped in Aunt Bear's lap.

"You look pretty," Ronald said.

"I like to eat wild roses," she answered, eating the petals off a stem as though it were a Popsicle or lollipop.

"I never heard of that," said Oliver, reaching for a rose of his own.

"I feel rosy and sweet inside when I swallow them," Aunt Bear said shyly.

"Guess I'll try one too. It sounds like a nice feeling." Ronald reached for a rose, cautiously removed one petal, and stuck it on his tongue. "Not bad," he said and plucked another petal.

"Maybe we should get to work on that peanut butter, Oliver," Aunt Bear said.

They gaped at her. "You knew?"

Laughing so hard the leaves on the nearby bushes shook, Aunt Bear clapped her paws together. "Oliver's carrying the jars to accommodate Ronald's insects, right?" She opened her pack and pulled out a book on trees, binoculars, and a large tin of fried apple rings coated with powdered sugar. "This is just-in-case food," she said, holding up a plastic bag filled with hard-boiled eggs.

"Just in case what?" They continued to stare, their arms limp in their laps.

"Just in case the woods and meadows have been picked clean by former campers." Aunt Bear plunged her paw into the peanut butter.

"Try some strawberry preserve," Oliver said, holding out the crock.

"Did you pack oranges?" Ronald asked as several rolled out of Oliver's pack.

"No, smart bear, they grew right here in a cellophane wrapper." He laughed and rolled in the grass. It felt marvelous eating real food and being smarter than Ronald. "There are some limes growing in the bottom of the pack."

"Oh good." Aunt Bear brushed sugar off her fur. "Limes are delicious with hickory nuts. Let's look out for some as we continue along. And Ronald, now that the jar is empty, you can look for specimens."

"How did you know?" Ronald tugged his ear.

"How did you know?" Oliver licked his lips.

Again Aunt Bear shook the leaves with her laughter. "I live outside, remember? I know how hungry you can get when you can't find a fish in the stream. I've passed too many bushes empty of berries when my stomach's been growling. And I wouldn't live outdoors if I didn't enjoy the company of birds." She held up the binoculars.

"Isn't camping supposed to be rough and rugged? Ma said Pa couldn't sleep once because of a gnarled root and you were all shivering and soggy because it poured. That sounds terrible. But I thought that's what camping is." Ronald didn't like to have to change his mind.

"Can be. But this bear likes her comfort and the outdoors. So I have an accommodation with Nature. I help her along with a jar of peanut butter, and I take shelter when she rains, either

in my house or under a tree umbrella, and
watch the drops flicker on the leaves.

Oliver and Ronald lolled on the bank, com-
fortable in the sound of Aunt Bear's voice.
Oliver thought she sounded like a thick-
trunked tree would if it could talk.

"And Nature pays me back with mounds of
rose bushes, sunsets that look like the sky's
been scalded, and feathery ferns that whish
against my legs as I walk through her woods."

They repacked their gear and walked along the brook path until the water widened gradually into a river. Every once in a while, one of them would shout, "Accommodation." Cradling the bag of eggs, Oliver kept his eye out for frogs for Ronald. Aunt Bear, with the binoculars around her neck, gathered nuts into a bag. And Ronald, relieved that the trip might be an expedition after all, walked briskly, with the books tucked under one arm and swinging the thermos in his other paw.

When they reached a clearing with large
rocks forming a crude fireplace, Aunt Bear held
up her paw. "This is it. Best fish in the river
right out there. You cubs unpack and start the
fire. And get ready for a fish feast. I can taste
them already!"

"Shall we sauté them, Aunt Bear? You didn't bring bread crumbs, did you?" Oliver asked.

Ronald and Aunt Bear laughed. "That's carrying accommodation too far, Master Chef. We'll just fry them over the fire."

"Sautéing is really frying, Aunt Bear. But it sounds more delicious."

"OK, sauté the fish. Now for some fun." She waded into the water until she was nearly waist-deep. The cubs watched from the bank. She didn't move a muscle. The water around her didn't even ripple. After a while, Oliver turned to Ronald and said, "The fire's just about perfect, and I've got the pan all ready."

"At least we have the just-in-case food," Ronald said. Suddenly they heard a whooshing sound, and Aunt Bear held up a flapping fish. "Got him, first try. Bring the pan, Ronald."

Ronald ran into the water and Oliver went back to his fire, patiently feeding it sticks until it flared up crackling and, he hoped, perfect for sautéing fish. Then he turned around and munched a handful of apple rings.

After they had eaten their fill, including
some eggs and the last of the preserves, they all
felt heavy with food and hiking. In a final spurt
of energy, they rolled out their sleeping bags
and curled into them, close to the flames of the
dying fire.

"I like your kind of camping, Aunt Bear,"
Oliver said, chewing the last apple ring, which
he had tucked into his sleeping bag for a snack.

"I love accommodation," sighed Ronald and
immediately fell fast asleep.

"What beautiful flowers. Where did you get the phlox? My favorite violets, oh Pa, look!" Ma was so happy, all her words tumbled together.

"Good catch, Aunt Bear." Pa held up the string of fish. "Bet you're all starving after a night in the woods. Did you have a good time?"

"We learned all about accommodation," Ronald said, "and we're not starving at all."

"I can still taste it," Oliver said, smacking his lips.

"Whatever are you talking about?" Ma asked, as she rubbed Oliver's back.

"It's how Aunt Bear goes camping." Oliver snuggled up to Ma.

Ronald tugged at Pa's paw. "Say there are these bears, say they start out on a hike, each for a different reason. Along the way, they figure out how to fit everybody's reason into the trip. That's accommodation."

Ma and Pa looked at each other.

"Aunt Bear caught the fish, I sautéed the fish, and Ronald got specimens for his laboratory." Oliver clapped his hands. "Now he'll leave Frank alone. That's accommodation."

Ronald bent over his pack and pulled out a jar. Inside, a small tree frog wriggled against the glass. "See these can-opener holes, Ma? That gave him enough air."

"What else is in that pack?"

"Just some tufts of moss"—he held out a large jar—"and these waterlilies, which won't be in your way. You love flowers, and these can float in a tank next to my fish."

Ma smiled. "And I suppose that's accommodation too?"

"It sure is," Oliver shouted. "You know, Ma, peanut-butter jars can hold more than peanut butter."